For Jill.
—LH

First published in the United States in 2023 by Sourcebooks

Text © 2022, 2023 by Juno Dawson
Illustrations © 2022, 2023 by Laura Hughes
Cover and internal design © 2023 by Sourcebooks

The illustrations were created using a
mixture of ink, gouache, and colored pencils.

Published by Sourcebooks Jabberwocky, an imprint of Sourcebooks Kids
P.O. Box 4410, Naperville, Illinois 60567-4410
(630) 961-3900
sourcebookskids.com

Originally published in 2022 in the UK by
Farshore, an imprint of HarperCollinsPublishers

Cataloging-in-Publication Data is on file with the Library of Congress.

Source of Production: China
Date of Production: November 2022
Run Number: 5028415

Printed and bound in China.
CH 10 9 8 7 6 5 4 3 2 1

YOU NEED TO Chill!

JUNO DAWSON

ILLUSTRATED BY LAURA HUGHES

sourcebooks
jabberwocky

Sometimes people say to me,
"What happened to your brother Bill?

We haven't seen him in ages.
Is he hiding?
Is he ill?"

"Is he lost in the park?

Is he scared of the dark?

Is he doing his homework still?"

That's when I look them in the eye and say,
"Hey, you need to chill."

"Was he eaten by a WHALE or SHARK?
Was he munched up just like krill?"

"That simply isn't true," I say.
"And, hey, you need to chill."

"Is he on vacation
in Barbados or Brazil?"

"No one has gone ANYWHERE...
And, hey, you need to chill."

"Is he at the zoo?

Is he at the fair?
Is he searching for a thrill?"

"Although we DO love the Ferris wheel...
Hey, you need to chill."

"But we're so confused!
And so concerned!
We cannot rest until..."

we find out what has happened

to your older brother Bill!"

"Did he tumble down and hurt himself?
Have they given him a pill?

Is he in the pool or on the field,
showing off his skill?

Was he taken to Mars by aliens?
Is he on their spaceship still?"

"Stop!" I say. "That's enough!
Hey, you need to chill."

WELCOME TO MARS

"There are NO hungry whales...

NO little green men...

Your hysteria is silly.

The truth is that my brother Bill...

Food

"...is now my sister Lily."

"It was maybe quite a shock, at first,
but she's really just the same.
She looks a little different
and she has a new first name."

"She's still clever and funny

and kind and cool.

She's one in a mil...

And if people have a problem, we shout...

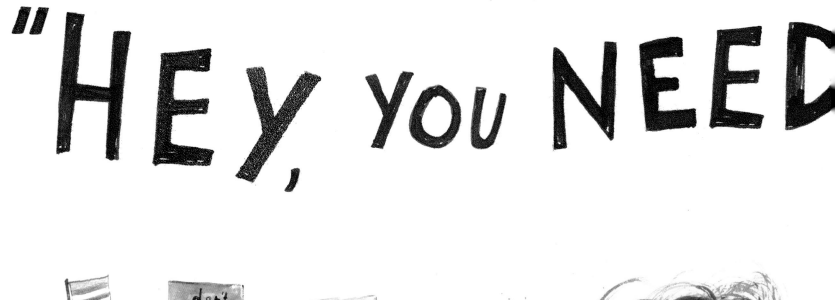

"HEY, YOU NEED

Gender Spectrum is a wonderful charity established in 2007 that works to create gender sensitive and inclusive environments for all children and teens. Their organization provides help for transgender, nonbinary, and gender-diverse kids, as well as support for their families.

More information can be found at:
genderspectrum.org